La-Ba Porridge

臘八粥

The Chinese call December of the lunar year "La-Yuae." On the 8th of December, every household has to prepare La-Ba porridge. Children, you might ask, "Why is it necessary to eat La-Ba porridge?" Well, there is a very interesting story to explain this tradition.

A long time ago, in the West Garden Temple of Suzhou City, there was a young monk named Number Six. He was a farmer's child, but because his family was too poor to raise him, he was sent to become a monk at a temple. At that time, the chief monk of the West Garden Temple recognized that Number Six was strong and honest. So, he sent Number Six to do chores in the kitchen.

West Garden Temple

　中國人稱農曆十二月爲臘月，臘月初八這天，在習俗上，家家戶戶都要煮「臘八粥」來吃。小朋友一定會問，爲什麼要吃「臘八粥」呢？原來，這其中含有一個很有意義的故事。

　很久很久以前蘇州的西園寺，有個叫阿六的小和尚他原是種田人家的孩子，因爲家裏很窮，父母便把他送來當和尚。當時西園寺的住持和尚，見阿六身體很健壯，人又忠厚老實，便派他到廚房做雜事。

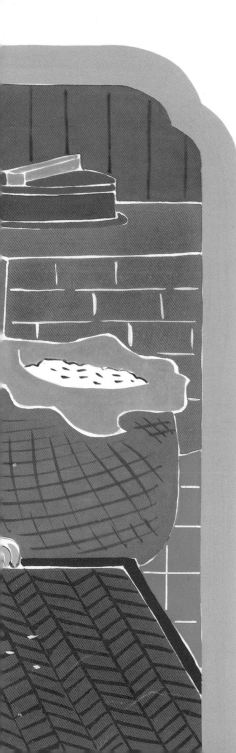

Everyday Number Six got up early and slept late. He was always busy with many chores: carrying water from the well, washing the rice and the vegetables, boiling water.... Sometimes, he even had to climb the mountains to gather firewood. He worked very hard.

Because he was born to a poor family, Number Six learned to be very thrifty. Every time he did the dishes, he always saved the few grains of leftover rice stuck to the bowls. He would put them on a mat to dry, then store them in a sack.

阿六每天起早睡晚，忙著挑水、淘米、洗菜、燒水……，有時還要上山撿柴，工作非常勤奮。

阿六生在窮苦人家，從小就有節儉的好習慣，他每次洗碗，都不忍心把剩下的飯粒倒掉，總是小心的把飯粒撈起來，攤在席子上曬乾，再用袋子裝起來。

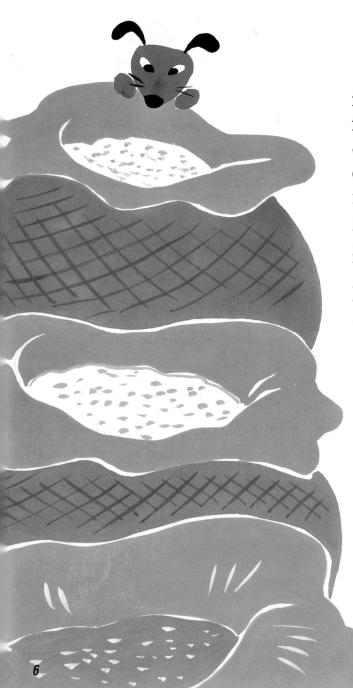

Even when burning the rice stalks in the fire, he checked carefully to make sure that there were no grains of rice left on them. If there were even one grain of rice, he would remove the stalk to salvage that grain. If he found one bean or one grain of wheat in the fields, he still brought it home and to save. Soon, his sack became filled with all kinds of grains.

燒火的時候，他也仔細檢查，看看那些用來燒火的稻桿子，還有沒有穀粒，哪怕只有一粒，他也要剝下穀殼收藏起來。平時他在田裏撿到一顆豆子、一粒麥子，也一樣要撿起來收藏，就這樣日積月累，他的袋子已經積下好多好多各式各樣的糧食了。

6

　　日子過得真快，轉眼就是臘月了。臘月初八
這天，是佛祖釋迦牟尼證道的佛日。西園寺的
和尚都聚在大殿裏念經、做法事。

　　阿六從柴房裏回來，正準備淘米煮飯，才發
現米缸空了，偏偏管糧的和尚還在念經，阿六
又不好去找他，因爲亂闖經堂是有罪的。

　　阿六左等右等，就是不見管糧的和尚來，眼
看就快中午了，若是誤了開飯的時間，阿六是
要挨罵的，這可怎麼辦呢！

The days passed very quickly, and soon it was December. Every 8th of December was the memorial day for the founder of Buddhism, Sakyamuni (563-483 B.C.), who came to preach people. All of the monks of the West Garden Temple would gather in the main temple to pray and to perform their ceremonies.

After coming back from the woodshed, Number Six was ready to make rice for lunch. Suddenly, he realized that the rice in the storage bin had been used up. The monk who was in charge of the food supply was busy praying. Number Six didn't want to interrupt him because it was a sin to disturb the monks while they were praying.

Number Six waited and waited for the monk who was in charge of the food supply to return. Lunch time was getting closer and closer. If Number Six didn't have the food ready on time, he was going to get scolded. What was he going to do?

Pacing back and forth, he scratched his head. He was very worried. Then, he spotted his sack of mixed-grains. Not worrying about how the food might taste, he poured all the grains that were in the sack into a pot to cook.

"Dong, dong, dong," the lunch bell rang. All the monks entered the dining hall. The monks stared at what was on the table. The food didn't look like porridge, and it didn't look like rice. They were puzzled.

阿六急得一會兒搔搔頭，一會兒跺跺腳。忽然間，他瞥見自己那口裝滿雜糧的袋子，他靈機一動，便把袋子裏的雜糧拿出來下鍋，至於好不好吃，他也顧不了了。

噹、噹、噹，開飯的鐘聲響了！和尚們走進齋堂一看，桌上擺的東西，粥不像粥，飯也不像飯，心裏覺得很納悶。

But because monks were not supposed to complain about what they received, they ate the strange food. Surprisingly, the food was pretty tasty. It satisfied their appetites. In no time at all, they finished all the food.

The chief monk asked Number Six, "What on earth did you cook today?"

Since Number Six was an honest boy, he told the chief monk the whole story. After the chief monk heard it, he smiled and said, "Well done. Because you value food, you save food. Because Number Six knew how to be thrifty, we were able to eat today. What a fine job, fine job."

Later when the monks heard about this, they all complimented Number Six on his thriftiness.

可是和尚們吃東西是不准挑剔的，於是，大家便悶著頭吃了起來，誰知一吃之下，才覺得味道滿不錯的，人人胃口大開，不到一會兒功夫，鍋底就朝了天。

住持和尚問阿六：「你今天燒的到底是什麼？」

阿六是老實人，便一五一十的把事實告訴住持。住持聽了，面露微笑，雙手合十說：「善哉、善哉，惜食有食，阿六積福，功德無量。」

和尚們聽說了這件事，都稱贊阿六勤儉節約。

From then on, everybody imitated Number Six by not wasting their food. When the 8th of December came around, everyone gathered all kinds of grains and made a porridge. Gradually, other people adopted this custom promoting thriftiness. So, whenever it's December the 8th, every household would use all kinds of different ingredients to make La-Ba porridge. Not only do people eat it to warm themselves up in the winter, but also to remind themselves to be thrifty.

La-Ba porridge

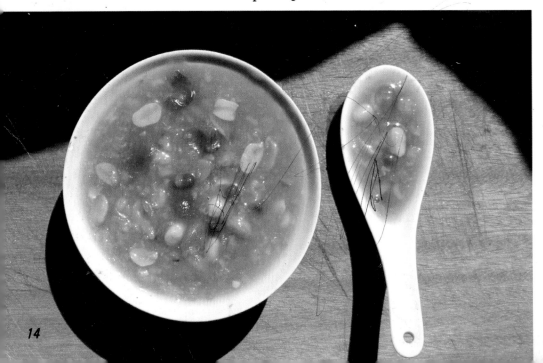

從此以後，大家都學阿六，處處珍惜糧食，每到臘月初八，就拿出來燒成粥吃。這種習慣，不久就傳到民間百姓，成為一種含有節儉意義的善良風俗。所以，每年臘月初八，家家戶戶都要燒一種用各式各樣材料煮成的「臘八粥」來吃。一方面，可以在寒冷的冬天暖暖身子；另方面，也是提醒大家要勤儉節約。

There is an old saying: When enjoying a meal, one must also appreciate the labor involved in its preparation. Number Six, who truly understood this message practice, tried to put it into whenever he could. Because of his good habit, he saved the day. This story advocates being thrifty and economical.

The reason why it is called "La-Ba" is because 'La' stood for December, and 'Ba' is the number 8 in Chinese. The recipe for La-Ba porridge usually includes rice, prunes, beans, peanuts, red beans, ... etc. After being made, it is first offered in a solemn ceremony to the deceased ancestors and gods. Then, it is served among the members of the family. In some areas, not only do people eat the porridge, but even dogs, cats, and other household pets eat it too. It is believed that by doing this, the upcoming year will bring better fortune and the pets will grow healthier.

15

The Stove God

灶王老爺

Whenever the lunar calendar's December 24th comes around, every household will make sweet rice balls to offer to the Hearth God in the kitchens. When he eats them, and his mouth becomes full with rice balls, he won't be able to go to heaven and speak badly about the people on earth. It has been said that this Protector of the hearth was originally a commoner from earth. How did he get to heaven and become a god of the stoves? Curiously though, if the kitchen is a place where people cooked meals, why would the Jade Emperor of Heavenly Gods place a god there? Well, the story happened this way...

每年到了農曆十二月二十四日，家家戶戶都會做甜湯圓來祭廚房裏的灶神，讓灶王爺吃了，塞著喉嚨，甜住嘴巴，到了天上，就不會給玉皇大帝打小報告，說人間的壞話。據說，這個灶王老爺本來也是凡間的人，後來為什麼升了天，做了廚房的神呢？最奇怪的是，廚房是燒飯做菜的地方，為什麼玉皇大帝會派個神坐鎮在那裏呢？原來是這樣的……

In the early days, there was a man named Chang Ding-Fu. He was very useless. Not only did he refuse to work to support his family, but he drank and gambled all day. He used up all of his inheritance and became bankrupt. He couldn't even afford to support his wife, Silver Flower. She didn't know what to do to survive. So, she decided to marry another man. Not having a place to live, nor food to eat, Chang Ding-Fu started wandering the streets and soon became a beggar.

One day, he bumped into Silver Flower. Silver Flower felt deeply sorry for him. She took him back to her new home to prepare him a nice home-made meal in the kitchen. After Chang Ding-Fu finished, he thought about how he hadn't been able to support his ex-wife. He was so ashamed that he couldn't even raise his head.

很早的時候，有一個叫張定福的人，非常不長進，不但不幹活兒賺錢養家，還成天喝酒賭錢，把家產都耗光了，最後成了窮光蛋，連老婆都養不起了。他的老婆叫銀花，沒法兒可想，只好改嫁別人。張定福沒房子住，沒東西吃，只好流浪街頭，成了叫化子。

　　有一天，正好給銀花碰見了，銀花可憐他沒飯吃，就帶他回現在丈夫的家，在灶房做了一頓好菜好湯招待他。張定福吃飽以後，想到自己連老婆都保不住，慚愧的直不起頭來。

At the same time, footsteps were heard from the doorway. Silver Flower got very nervous and said, "Oh no! My husband is back! He's very jealous. You'd better hide before he sees you!"

The only place that he could hide in the kitchen was in the big stove. Chang Ding-Fu didn't even have time to think. He just stuck his head into the stove.

這時候，門口突然響起啪達啪達的腳步聲。銀花臉色大變，慌張的說：「糟了！我丈夫回來了！他的醋勁很大，你趕快躲起來，別讓他看見！」

灶房裏只有一個大灶可以躲人，張定福來不及想，就一頭鑽進去。

才剛躲好，銀花的丈夫就跨進灶房，凶霸霸的喊著：「銀花，還不快去打桶水來給老爺我洗臉！」銀花怕丈夫懷疑，轉身就離開灶房去打水。

銀花的丈夫突然覺得口乾，水壺卻沒半滴水，他一邊罵銀花，一邊打開灶門，拿了幾根木柴丟進去，點了火，準備燒開水。柴劈哩啪拉燒了起來，躲在灶裏的張定福屏著氣，不敢吭聲，他怕被銀花的丈夫發現，害了銀花。

火苗越來越大，燒到張定福的鞋子、衣服……就這樣，張定福活活被燒死了。

銀花打水回來，一看灶裏升了火，知道張定福已經被燒成灰了，忍不住掉下眼淚。

As he just finished climbing in, Silver Flower's husband came into the kitchen and hollered, "Silver Flower! Hurry and go get some water from the well for me to wash my face!" Silver Flower was afraid that he might get suspicious. So, she turned and left the kitchen to get the water.

All of a sudden, Silver Flower's husband felt thirsty, but there was no water in the pot. While still yelling at Silver Flower, he opened the stove door and threw in some wood. He lit the fire to boil some water. The wood started to crackle and burn. Chang Ding-Fu, who was hiding in the stove, held his breath. He didn't dare to say a word. He was afraid Silver Flower's husband might find out and therefore punish her.

The flames got bigger and bigger. It started burning Chang Ding-Fu's shoes, his clothes... In this way, Chang Ding-Fu was burned to death.

When Silver Flower came back from drawing water, she saw that the fire was lit in the stove. Then, she knew Chang Ding-Fu had passed away. Tears rolled silently down her face.

從這天開始，銀花每天做飯看到大灶，就會想起為她死掉的張定福。她越想越傷心，就偷偷的替張定福立一個牌位，放在灶頭，早晚祭拜他。

左右鄰居看到銀花每天那麼虔誠的在廚房拜拜，覺得很奇怪，就問她在拜什麼東西。銀花怕人家發現她的秘密，就隨便撒了一個謊。「我拜的是灶神！咱們每天都在這個大灶做飯燒菜的，當然應該拜拜他謝謝他咯！」大家聽了，覺得很有道理，就學起銀花拜起灶神來。

From that day and on, every time Silver Flower saw the large stove, she would think of Chang Ding-Fu. The more she thought about him, the sadder she became. Secretly, she set up a memorial shrine for him on top of the stove to pray for him day and night.

Neighbors who saw Silver Flower praying so faithfully in the kitchen thought it strange. They asked her why she prayed there. As she didn't want anyone to find out her secret, she said, "I am worshipping the God of the hearth. We cook on this large stove everyday. Naturally, we should worship him and thank him." After everyone heard this, they all felt it made sense. So, they started to worshipping the "Stove God" just like Silver Flower.

Stove **God and S**tove Goddess

These events were soon noticed by the Jade Emperor of Heavenly Gods. He remembered Chang Ding-Fu's goodness just before Chang's death. So, the Jade Emperor officially appointed him) as the Stove God. But to punish him for not being a good man during his whole lifetime, the god made him write down everyone's good and bad deeds everyday. At the end of every year, he had to take the list to heaven and report it to the Jade Emperor. This is why we send the Stove God to heaven every December 24th and use sweet rice balls to win his favor.

這件事，不久就被天上的玉皇大帝知道了。玉皇大帝念張定福死前的一點善心，就正式派他做了灶房的神。不過，為了罰他生前不好好做人，規定他每天要記下每家做的好事和壞事，在每年年尾，到天上跟他報告。這就是每年十二月二十四日送灶神上天，和用甜湯圓甜他嘴巴的由來。

It has been that on the left and right side of the Stove God there are 2 other assistant gods. One carries a good-deed jar and the other carries a bad-deed jar. They record what every family does during the year and take the list up to the head god at the end of the year.

From the worship of the Stove God, we can see that in China many kinds of gods and ancestors are honored. The Chinese believe that every human action is recorded by the gods. Therefore, we should not dare to commit any sins. But as humans are not perfect, mistakes are still made. That's how the custom of offering sweet rice balls for penance came about.

Chinese Children's Stories **series** consists of 100 volumes; 20 titles of subjects grouped in 5-book sets.

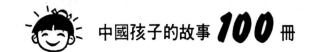

中國孩子的故事 **100** 冊

First edition for the United States
published in 1991 by Wonder Kids Publications
Copyright © Emily Ching and Ko-Shee Ching 1991
Edited by Emily Ching, Ko-Shee Ching, and Dr. Theresa Austin
Chinese version first published 1988 by
Hwa-I Publishing Co.
Taipei, Taiwan, R.O.C.
All rights reserved.
All inquiries should be addressed to:
Wonder Kids Publications
P.O. Box 3485
Cerritos, CA 90703
International Standard Book No. 1-56162-030-0
Library of Congress Catalog Card No. 90-60797
Printed in Taiwan